Sheila C. Morgan

Illustrated by Zee Graphic Tones

XULON PRESS

2301 Lucien Way #415
Maitland, FL 32751
407.339.4217
www.xulonpress.com

Printed in the United States of America.

ISBN-13: 978-1-6312-9071-8

I dedicate this book to my granddaughter Isadora Skye, who is as sweet as honey pie.

Love Granna

When I'm with my family or my
teacher and friends at school,
they call me Izzy and that's okay.
But I have other friends in my
pretend garden, who know me
when I come out to play.

In the summer when I lie awake at night, I visit my friends even when they are out of sight. Like the night I said, what if I was Izzy the bee, would I still be able to bend my knee.

Soon after, Mom and Dad
said, Izzy
it's time to go to bed.
We prayed,
and then on my pillow, I
snuggled my head.

Before I knew it, I was flying around a huge hive with bees. Then I told them, "Come out here and play with me please." The bees seemed to all be sleeping, so in my big voice I said.

"Get up, get up,
sleeping bees and
get out of bed."

They all flew out, yes every little bee, and all our wings were fluttering, as far as I could see.

Then we took off flying,
I knew not where, and suddenly
I said, "hey friends;
I have something for
you to hear."

Can you imagine God looking
at us swirling round and round?
He knows each one of us and
even how we sound. What a
sight we must be! Come on my
friends, won't you go on a
little trip with me?

All the bees said, how far
can we go?
Busy Izzy, it's still dark
you know?
No need to worry, come now,
just hurry.

God wants us to live by faith and not by sight and His vision will guide us, even in the darkness of night. You know God can see us and He made us all.

We're down here on earth,
that's shaped like a great big
ball. We can't see the bottom
and we can't see the top. We're
just spinning around and round,
never knowing where we
will stop.

God made us little worker bees, and He hears our busy buzzing sound, while we're making sweet honey to spread all around. From one day to the next, I think it must be a test, to see which busy bee will do our very best.

We are only here for a season, and God's plan is the reason. Like the Queen Bee, doing her thing, she's a special creation of the King of Kings. Working for the Sweetest Honey in the Rock, always knowing what time it is, without the help of a clock.

Our God is a great big God,

bigger than all His creation, and every day we can have great expectation. I thank him so much for my life as a tiny little bee, showing how awesome He is and still cares about tiny little me. Here with my friends, I'm happy, Izzy busy little bee, and look; we can all bow our knee.

So, In the name of Jesus before
we fly back to our beehive,
let's pray and thank God
that we are alive.

BBBBUUUUZZZZZZZZZZZZZZZZZ.
BBBBUUUUZZZZZZZZZZZZZZZZZ.
BBBUUUUZZZZZZZZZZZZZZZZZ.
BBBBUUUUZZZZZZZZZZZZZZZZZ.
BBBBUUUUZZZZZZZZZZZZZZZZZ.

Good morning Izzy,
it's time to wake up.

Sheila C. Morgan has developed honor and great appreciation to God for the gift and passion to write. Her desire to reach children in their early developmental years and experience the awareness of God, sparked many ideas to incorporate in a child's everyday learning experiences. Her writing background expands from several categories during her career and ministry. Through it all, Sheila believes no matter what, God always has a plan. Happy to introduce her children's book "Izzy Busy Bee", encourages her optimistic view, to continue serving in the body of Christ and love for children and their future.